Sweet & Sour Lily

Sweet & Sour Lily

by Sally Warner

illustrated by
Jacqueline Rogers

SCHOLASTIC INC.
New York Toronto London Auckland Sydney
Mexico City New Delhi Hong Kong

ISBN 0-439-09349-X

Text copyright © 1998 by Sally Warner.
Illustrations copyright © 1998 by Jacqueline Rogers.
All rights reserved.
Published by Scholastic Inc., 555 Broadway, New York, NY 10012,
by arrangement with Alfred A. Knopf, Inc. SCHOLASTIC and
associated logos are trademarks and/or registered
trademarks of Scholastic Inc.

12 11 10 9 8 7 6 5 4 3   0 1 2 3 4/0

Printed in the U.S.A.   40

First Scholastic printing, October 1999

For Missy Maxwell

CONTENTS

Sweet & Sour Lily

CHAPTER ONE
Because

"LaVon and Daisy hate this show," I inform Casey. He is my brother. Just because he's twelve years old and I am six, he thinks he's so great.

Mommy sighs, and Case makes a snorty sound. "I'm tired of hearing about LaVon and Daisy, LaVon and Daisy," he says to me. "Big deal, Lily—so you made two new friends your first week of school. Can't you talk about something else? And anyway, we always watch this show on Sunday night."

I turn around from where I am sitting cross-legged on the rug and stare at my

mommy, who is in the big soft chair behind me. I am waiting for her to tell Case to stop picking on me, but she just sighs again. She is barely even watching this stupid TV show.

Oops! When I turn around to look at Mommy, I knock over Growler, Mr. Fluff, and Tiger Annie, who were sitting in a line, also watching TV. They are my three favorite stuffed animals. "Now look what you made me do," I say to Case.

"Shhh, it's on again," Case tells me. He is sprawled on the rug, his long arms and legs going every which way, like he just fell out of bed.

"So what," I mutter, but then I am quiet. I sit my animals up straight again so they can see.

What Case said is not true, that I have two new friends. I wish!

Daisy Greenough and LaVon Hamilton are the most fun girls in my new first-grade class, and they are friends with each other. I am friends with nobody, at least not yet.

This is because I am a brand-new kid at Betsy Ross Primary School here in Philadelphia, where everyone knows each other but no one knows me.

I am brand-new because we had to move here from Cherry Hill, New Jersey, where we lived in a house. Now we live in an apartment, where you have to climb stairs all the time.

We had to move because my daddy went away, and my mommy had to get a job.

My daddy went away because the judge said he did something wrong.

The judge said that, because he thinks my daddy and another man took some things that didn't belong to them. So he sent them to jail. But don't tell, because we are keeping that a secret.

I don't know what I think, except that I miss my daddy.

And I miss our old house.

And I miss having friends.

"There, it's over, you'll be glad to know," Case sighs, rolling over onto his back. "Tell LaVon and Daisy how great it was! They're missing a very good show."

"Shut up," I tell him. I say it very softly, though, so my mommy won't hear. She doesn't like us to use bad words.

But when I turn around to peek at Mommy, I see that she has fallen asleep in the chair.

Again.

"Shut up," I say a little louder. I want Mommy to wake up so she can tell me to take a bath and then tuck me in. That's what mommies are supposed to do!

"*You* shut up," Case tells me, and he stretches and yawns.

I grab Mr. Fluff, and I bop Case on the head with him. It serves Case right!

"Give me that!" Case yells, and he starts pulling on Mr. Fluff's tail. He is a cat, by the way. Mr. Fluff is, not Casey.

"Quit it!" I holler, and then I make a yowly sound that is part me and part Mr. Fluff.

Mommy wakes up.

"Case is trying to wreck Mr. Fluff," I shout. "And he's being mean about Daisy and LaVon, too!"

"I am *not*," Case says, and he lets go of Mr. Fluff's tail so fast that I roll backwards. I almost do a somersault.

Mommy frowns. "Case," she says, "don't pick on Lily's new friends, honey." She gives him a special glance, like she is telling him a secret.

This makes me madder than ever. "Stop *looking* that way!" I yell—at both of them. Then I run into the bathroom with Mr. Fluff and slam the door behind me.

Because I can't think of anything else to do.

CHAPTER TWO
Sweet and Sour

Do you think that Lily Hill sounds like a famous name? You will someday, because that's my name, and I will be a star. But like I told you, right here and right now nobody knows my name.

My daddy calls me Lily-baby on the phone, but I'm *not* a baby. I turned six last summer, right before we moved to the city.

I hate Philadelphia. It smells bad. But I love my daddy. He smells good, I remember. Like shoe polish, which is number one of my three favorite smells. Here are the other two:

2. Gasoline.

3. Chocolate chip cookies when they are still in the oven.

Sometimes my mommy calls me sweetie pie. If I was a pie, I would be the yellow kind with fluffy stuff on top like a big white hat. Everyone would see me coming when I walked down the street. But I am *not* a pie!

I am trying to be sweet, though, ever since we moved. Mommy said it was important for all of us to make a new start here.

I loved kindergarten at my old school, but I was a sour-puss at the end of the year. I heard the playground lady say so. "She's such a little sour-puss lately," she said. She was right, but like Stevie

Braddock says at my new school, it was nobody's beeswax why.

This other lady said, "She used to be so darling. Maybe it's just a phase."

I asked my brother Case what that meant. He said that a phase is something you go through, so I guess it is kind of like a door.

When I started going to my new school last week, I decided it was time to be a sweet-puss, not a sour-puss. I want to be darling again! Someday I will be the cutest person at Betsy Ross Primary School. All the kids will like me.

The trouble now is, they already like each other. That means there is no room for them to like me. Almost all of them were in kindergarten together, and I think I am the only new kid in the whole class.

During recess they play-play-play together like crazy. I stand next to the fence and think about what I will do when I am famous.

Someday I will be the most beautiful teenager there ever was. My curly hair will hang all the way down to my feet. I will also be a ballerina. I will dance right past the Betsy Ross School for Very Mean Kids, and I will twirl and laugh.

But now, during recess, LaVon plays with Daisy. Stevie plays with Marcus. And I just stand there looking stupid.

I am still acting sweet, though. I sit up straight in class and never bother my neighbor. Everyone at my old school

would be so surprised, because I was the queen of bothering my neighbor there. But I couldn't help it. It wasn't my fault! Those were my sour-puss days, remember.

My new teacher's name is Ms. Marshall, and I think she likes me. I am nice and quiet, and I always smile, no matter how much smiling hurts my face. Who wouldn't like that?

I told Case my plan about being sweet at my brand-new school and he said, "Huh, good luck." He said that in a funny way, like he didn't really mean it. Then he told me anyone could be good the first week of school, even me, but after that it gets tougher. So I guess this week I will have to try extra hard.

Maybe Case thinks I can't do it, but I know I can.

It's hard making a new start, and it's hard making new friends, too. But sitting here on the bathroom floor, I'm starting to get a secret idea. . . .

CHAPTER THREE
Secret

Here is my secret idea. I heard Daisy and LaVon talking about their Barbie dolls and all the clothes they wear. Well, I have a Barbie doll too! And I could bring her with me to school.

Her name isn't Barbie, though, it's Lilanna, which is a much more beautiful name. I added it together out of two names—*Lily,* which is me, and *Anna,* which is what I *wish* my name was. Why should I let somebody else name my doll?

I would never bring my stuffed animals to school, by the way. That is not a first-grade thing to do. In my opinion.

Anyway, last week was my first week at stinky Betsy Ross Primary School. When it was finally over, Mommy brought me a present for being such a good sport. It was a new outfit for Lilanna! The outfit has four parts to it:

1. A glittery skirt.
2. A red fuzzy sweater.
3. A tiny golden belt.
4. Bright red shoes.

The outfit is for when Lilanna goes to a party, which is almost every night. Case helped me punch through the plastic. It was as hard as a brick, but we finally got the clothes out. They fit her perfectly.

So like I said, my idea is that I will bring Lilanna to school. She will be all dressed up in her new outfit and I will show her to

Daisy and LaVon. They will love her new clothes so much that they will probably want to start playing with me right away!

But there is a first-grade rule that is getting in the way of my plan. Here is the stupid rule: Do not bring toys to class.

At my old school we were allowed to bring one toy to class every Friday, as long as we shared. But I was in kindergarten then.

At my new school there are so many rules that I can't even remember them, and that makes me nervous. What if I break a rule by mistake? Like what if there is a first-grade rule at Betsy Ross that says no humming, and I hum by accident? I will get busted. *Bus-ted*—that's what Stevie Braddock says at my new school.

The only rules here that I can remember are these:

1. Do not run in the hallways.
2. Do not talk when someone else is already talking.
3. Do not bring toys to class.

I will not run in the hallways, and I will not talk when someone else is talking, even if I have something much better to say. But I *have* to bring Lilanna to class.

I won't really be taking her to *class*, though, just to the cloakroom. She will go in my backpack. Then when Daisy and LaVon come in to hang up their stuff, I can take Lilanna out and show her to them.

That is the other thing. The no-toys rule is so that kids won't play at school when they should be working, but we won't *play* with Lilanna. We'll just look at her. So it doesn't really count, does it?

Even though I won't be doing anything wrong, I don't think I'm going to tell Mommy or Case about my plan. That's the *secret* part.

So tomorrow is the first day of my second week in the first grade at Betsy Ross. Case said that from now on it will be hard for me to be good. But not only am I going to stay all smiley and sweet for Ms. Marshall this week, I am also going to make friends with Daisy and LaVon.

I can't wait for tomorrow!

"Okay, I'm coming out of the bathroom now!" I yell. I just hope that someone is paying attention, that's all.

CHAPTER FOUR
Two Little Flowers

Daisy has a backpack with zebra stripes on it. And LaVon's backpack is just like a teddy bear. It is fuzzy, and it even has a head and paws!

My backpack used to be Case's backpack. It smells like old peanut butter sandwiches in there, and I hate it. Mommy says she didn't even know I would need a backpack in the first grade, and maybe I will get a new one for Christmas. I hope so.

I put lots of things in my backpack. Here is what is in there now:

1. A sweater to wear in the classroom after I take off my jacket.
2. Extra socks for when my feet get wet.
3. Red sneakers for when I take off my rain boots.

And in case you didn't figure it out yet, guess what's underneath all these things?

4. Lilanna.

Yes, I am really going to do it! But first it's time for breakfast. I always have cereal. It's my favorite.

"Lily, take smaller bites," my mommy says. "You're going to spill."

"Norf nert," I say, and a few flakes fly out onto the table.

"Yes, you are," she says, "and don't talk with your mouth full." She is reading the newspaper and stirring her coffee, *clink clink*.

I swallow my bite of cereal. "Where's Case?" I ask, looking around. In our apartment the kitchen is at one end of the living room. Case sleeps at the other end of the room, in a hidey-hole with a curtain in front. Whenever I want to talk to him, I have to stand next to the curtain and say "Knock, knock!" I pretend it is a door.

But now the curtain is open and Case is gone.

"He left early," Mommy says. "He still doesn't trust the city bus to get him there on time." Case just started a new school too.

"Huh," I say, and I load up my spoon again.

"Smaller bites," Mommy reminds me.

I dump most of the spoonful back into the bowl. Then I try to slurp a tiny bite in where my front teeth are missing. It doesn't work, but it tickles.

"You're making a mess," Mommy says.

"I'm eating tiny bites just like you told me to," I say. And I smile so she won't think I'm arguing.

Mommy folds up her paper and sighs. "Well, if you're playing with your food, you must be done. Go and brush your teeth, sweetie."

Yippee! I am happy to do this, because after tooth-brushing comes walking to school, and you know what will happen after that.

"I'm so glad you're feeling better

about school this week," Mommy says as we slosh down the sidewalk. I am all covered up in my raincoat, my rain hat, and my boots. I look like a piece of leftover meatloaf all wrapped up in plastic, but at least I am cozy and warm.

And so is Lilanna!

"Bye, baby," Mommy says when we get to school. After she walks a few more blocks, she will be at work.

"Bye," I say, looking up the steps. The bell must be about to ring, and I have to get to the cloakroom on time. If I don't, my secret plan will be ruined! "Well, bye," I say again.

Mommy laughs. "I can take a hint," she says. She gives me a hug and walks away. I don't see her do this, though, because I am already running up the front steps of the school.

The noise in the hall at this school is so loud you can't believe it. Some big kids are yelling and shoving, and you just have to stay out of their way, or else. I scoot to my classroom as fast as I can without running in the hallways.

Good! Daisy isn't here yet. I wait for her in the cloakroom, trying to look busy. I *s-l-o-w-l-y* hang up my jacket, my raincoat, and my rain hat on the hook next to LaVon's bear. My rain clothes look like a floppy little person waiting for me.

Then I *s-l-o-w-l-y* take off my boots. I reach inside my backpack to get my sneakers. Stevie Braddock and this other kid,

Marcus, are busy going through their lunch sacks. "I've got cookies," Stevie says.

"Well, I've got a cupcake from my little sister's birthday party," Marcus says. He takes it out of his sack. "Want to trade?" My mouth starts to water. I love birthday party food. The frosting is all smooshy, but it still looks good.

"Why do you want to trade a cupcake?" Stevie asks. "What's wrong with it?"

"Nothing," Marcus says. "But I already ate five of them at the party yesterday."

"Okay, I'll trade," Stevie says. "As long as it doesn't have nuts in it. I'm allergic." But he acts like his fingers are glued to the cookie bag, it takes him so long to let go. Then he turns and makes a face at me. "Hey, what are you staring at?" he asks.

"Nothing," I whisper.

"Well, quit it," he says. "Mind your own beeswax."

Just then Daisy comes rushing into the cloakroom. Her face is all pink because she's almost late. She starts to hang up her raincoat.

I reach into my backpack like I am getting out a snack, but instead I pull out Lilanna. "Look what I brought," I say to Daisy, and I show her Lilanna. I pretend it's no big deal, but Lilanna looks beautiful.

Daisy smiles a little and takes Lilanna in her hand. This is the first time Daisy has really noticed me. She looks at Lilanna's pretty new clothes.

"Her name is Lilanna, not Barbie," I say.

"And you can make her belt bigger or smaller."

Daisy touches the belt with one finger. She has a greedy look on her face, like the belt is a shiny little snack. "Huh," Daisy says.

I am starting to get scared. What if Ms. Marshall finds us holding a doll? "Well, we better go sit down," I say to Daisy. I hold out my hand for Lilanna.

"No," Daisy says, and she holds on tight to my doll. She pushes herself back against the raincoats like she's melting. "I want to show LaVon," she says.

"You can't," I say. "She's already sitting down."

"I'll show her at lunch, then," Daisy says, and she whirls around and stuffs

Lilanna into her zebra-striped backpack. "Don't worry. I'll give her back later," she says.

"Give it now," I say. I am trying not to cry. It would be terrible to cry! "Come on," I say, "it's mine."

"What's yours?" a voice asks, and Daisy and I look up. It is Ms. Marshall, and she is frowning.

I take a deep, shaky breath. "She took my—my—" But I can't finish what I am saying, because I don't want to get in trouble for bringing a toy to school.

"I took her raisins," Daisy says all of a sudden, and she reaches into her backpack for a little box. "I'm sorry. I was only teasing," she says. She's such a good liar! But I hate her, because she stole Lilanna.

Ms. Marshall takes the box of raisins and gives them to me. "Here you go," she says. "Now you two sit down and be nice to each other. I can't have Lily and Daisy fighting. My two little flowers!"

There is nothing I can do, so I go sit down.

But I'm not a little flower, and I *hate* raisins.

CHAPTER FIVE
Busted!

After we have practiced writing numbers for about a hundred years, it is time for nutrition break. In kindergarten this was just called snack time, but it is the exact same thing. Nutrition break is so kids don't starve before lunch.

Today, though, we have to eat our nutrition in the classroom, because it's still raining. Ms. Marshall stands in the middle of the cloakroom and watches us while we get our snacks. This is so we don't get carried away and eat our entire lunch, she says.

That would be a disaster, because first grade doesn't get out until two-thirty. I liked it better in kindergarten, where you could go home and eat a normal lunch in your own kitchen. Mommy didn't have a job then. Also, my daddy still lived at home.

No way am I going to eat those sticky raisins, but I'm not giving them back to Daisy, either. So I put them in my backpack and take out some peanut butter celery. Daisy is standing right next to me. She whispers to LaVon, and then they both look at me. I pretend I don't see them.

I can't be mean to Daisy with Ms. Marshall standing right there, and Daisy can't show LaVon my doll, and Ms. Marshall isn't leaving. Finally we all go back to our seats to eat our snacks.

The peanut butter is sticking to the inside of my mouth. I make a *kuh kuh kuh* sound. "Lily, would you like to be excused to go get a drink of water?" Ms. Marshall asks.

I give her a peanut-buttery smile and nod my head *yes.* Then I go out into the hall.

The silver drinking fountain is cold and sweaty, and it makes a funny humming noise. Also, the water tastes weird, and someone has spit out some wrinkly green gum where the water splashes. But I have to do something about the *kuh kuh kuh*, so I hold my nose and try to take a drink.

I keep peeking at Ms. Marshall's door the whole time. I hope that Daisy will come out to get a drink or to use the girls' restroom, and then I can yell at her about Lilanna. Maybe I will even pound her a little. I will yell and pound quietly, though, because I don't want to get in trouble.

But instead of Daisy coming out, Ms. Marshall pokes her head out the door. She says, "Lily, are you planning on joining us anytime soon?"

"Yes," I say, and I wipe my drippy mouth on my sleeve. I follow her into the class. It is time for us to look at pictures of things with words under them. We do this for about another hundred years, and then it is time for lunch.

Finally.

"Boys and girls," Ms. Marshall says, "because of the weather, you will be eating in the cafeteria today, instead of on the playground, even if you brought your lunch from home."

"Yay-y-y!" everybody yells. I don't know why, because we already know that our school cafeteria is the noisiest, stickiest place in the whole city. Worse than that, almost all the kids who eat there are bigger than us first graders. It's like we're the babies, so we have to huddle together like kittens in a basket, even if we hate each other.

But sometimes we all yell "Yay-y-y!" just because it's fun to yell "Yay-y-y." It makes it seem like something interesting is happening.

I know all about how kittens in a basket look, by the way, because of our old neighbors in Cherry Hill. They had kittens in a basket. Their cat did, I mean.

One good thing about eating in the cafeteria is that we kids don't have to put on our outside clothes to go there. We all scramble back to the cloakroom. "Leave your backpacks here, girls and boys," Ms. Marshall calls out. "Only take your lunches!"

I stand next to Daisy in the cloakroom and watch her as she paws through her striped backpack for her lunch. "Give me my doll," I growl at her.

"Later, after lunch," she says. "I didn't get a chance to show LaVon yet."

LaVon is unzipping her bear. She pulls out a bright green lunch sack. LaVon has really cool stuff.

"I don't care," I say to Daisy. "Give it!" I can't remember why I ever wanted to be friends with Daisy and LaVon in the first place.

Ms. Marshall is in the cloakroom clapping her hands for attention. Her hair is coming out of its ponytail, and her face is all pink. "Boys and girls!" she says. "Girls and boys!" Ms. Marshall tries to be fair. Sometimes she puts the boys first, but sometimes she puts the girls first.

We all have our lunches now. "Give me back my doll," I whisper to Daisy.

"No," she whispers back.

"Line up, everyone," Ms. Marshall says. "I will walk you to the cafeteria." I look hard at Daisy's backpack. I can almost see Lilanna inside it! I wish I had x-ray eyes.

I also wish I could stay behind and hide in the cloakroom until everyone is gone. Then I could get my doll back for sure.

But Ms. Marshall is marching us down the hall. "Quietly, everyone," she says.

In front of me Stevie and Marcus are shoving each other. "This is you," Stevie says, and he makes a face at Marcus. I try to remember the face so I can make it at Case later on.

"Oh, yeah?" Marcus says. "Well, this is *you!*" And he makes an even better face. I'll have to practice that one. Marcus can almost touch the bottom of his chin with his tongue.

Ms. Marshall starts to say something to them, but we have reached the cafeteria. And she smiles big, because her first-grade class is someone else's problem now. At least for a little while.

I sit across the table from Daisy and LaVon. I don't look at them, but I can tell they are whispering and giggling together. I pretend I don't care. I pretend that my tuna sandwich is the most interesting thing in the world.

I like tuna sandwiches the way my mommy fixes them, but nobody else. She makes them on soft white bread, because I hate bread with bumps in it. And she doesn't put anything funny in with the tuna.

Besides the sandwich, here are the other things in my lunch:

2. Carrot strips cut skinny.

3. A piece of string cheese.

4. Two oatmeal cookies, with *no raisins* in them.

5. A box of apple juice that you poke a straw into.

After lunch, I stuff all my empty bags back into the lunch sack and get up to throw it away. But the trash cans in our cafeteria are terrible. You should see them! They are always crammed so full that nothing fits inside without a fight. They look like someone dumped bowls of goop over the tops of them, so when you try to jam in your trash, you get all icky.

I don't see Daisy and LaVon anymore. I go to the stupid restroom to wash my smelly hands. I wish I could take a rest somewhere, too, but that part is a big fat lie.

Back in the cloakroom, where some kids are taking off sweaters or putting on sweaters, Daisy is finally ready to give me my doll back. I guess she and LaVon have finished looking at her. "Thanks *a lot*," I say, so that they know I don't mean it.

But Lilanna looks different. Her perfect hair is all messed up, for one thing, and her red fuzzy sweater has a smudge on it. Also, one of her shoes is missing. "It fell off in the hall, and we couldn't find it," Daisy says. "I'm sorry."

I give her a mean look. I already know what a good liar she is, so maybe she is lying now!

"I'm sorry, too," LaVon says. "She's really pretty, though. I love her belt."

"Huh," I say. My eyes feel hot, like tears might start popping out. Lilanna doesn't look so special to me anymore. Even her belt doesn't sparkle as much as it did this morning.

"Lily?" a voice says.

I look up, and guess who is watching me? Ms. Marshall, and she has a serious expression on her face.

No fair!

What is she doing in the cloakroom?

Why isn't she standing at her desk getting ready for the afternoon?

I try to hide Lilanna behind my back. "Give me the doll," Ms. Marshall says, and she holds out her hand.

I can't move. Everyone in the cloakroom is watching me.

"Lily," Ms. Marshall says again, "you know the rule. What happened when Stevie brought his action figure to class?"

"You took it away," I mumble.

"And what happened when Marcus brought that little car?"

"You took it," I say again. *Oh, great,* I think. Now instead of being Sweet Lily at my brand-new school, I get to be a member of the bad-boys club.

"Yes," Ms. Marshall says, "I took those toys because Stevie and Marcus broke the rule. And rules are for girls as well as boys. The first grade is a place for work, not play. Now give me the doll, please. You'll get it back on Friday after school."

I start to say something. "But I didn't—" I can't finish.

"You didn't what, Lily?" Ms. Marshall asks me.

"Oh, nothing," I say. "Here." And I slap the doll into Ms. Marshall's hand. "Take it," I tell her.

If Ms. Marshall is surprised that I can be so rude, she doesn't show it. She walks to the front of the class, opens a drawer in her desk, and puts Lilanna inside where she can barely breathe.

She locks the drawer—and Lilanna didn't do a single solitary thing that was wrong.

I was the one.

Everyone is quiet. They step aside when I go to sit down, and some of them whisper. *Lily, Lily, Lily,* I hear.

Daisy and LaVon sit down, too. Daisy

turns around in her chair. *"I'm sorry,"* she says with her mouth not making any noise.

I look away. Who even cares?

I can feel a sour look spread across my face.

CHAPTER SIX
Even More Trouble

This is going to be the longest afternoon in my whole life so far. Everyone else is work-work-working. They are minding their own beeswax, even Stevie and Marcus.

I am only pretending to work, but I feel like bothering every single one of my neighbors with a big old stick. *Fwap!* I'd hit all the desks like they were drums.

At least I don't have to smile all the time anymore. My face was getting sore. Now that I am in trouble I can frown all I want to. I practice my frowniest face.

"Lily? Do you need to be excused?"

Ms. Marshall says. This is the polite way of asking if I need to go potty.

"Yes," I say.

"Well, be sure and come back as soon as you're done," Ms. Marshall says.

"Okay," I say, and I hurry out of the room before she can change her mind.

One of the girls' restrooms at Betsy Ross School for the Stinky is just down the hall from our class. I try not to use it during recess or lunch, though, except for washing my hands. But I don't like going potty when other kids are in the same room as me. It is very embarrassing, I think. And it's not just other little kids in there. It can be fourth- or fifth-grade girls, too. *Big* ones.

Also, I hate the way the restroom smells

like squirty bubble-gum soap, and those rough brown paper towels hurt your hands. So I try not to use the restroom at school, and sometimes I have a stomach-ache by the time I go to child care.

But it is pretty cool being in the restroom all by myself. After I use one toi-let, I flush the other three just to make sure the flushers work. Now the girls' restroom sounds like an airplane that is about to take off!

That's the only good thing about school restrooms, the echoes. I decide to test the two soap squirters, too. "Hmm, these work pretty good," I say in a loud, booming voice. The smelly pink soap dribbles down the edges of the sink.

Uh-oh, now I have to clean up the soap.

"What a mess," I scold, sounding very mean. "Better get some of those towels."

The paper towels hang down like big flappy tongues. I start pulling on them. *One, two, three* from one towel box, and *one, two, three* from the other. Now I have six paper towels. Hey, I'm doing some arithmetic here! Ms. Marshall would be proud and happy, I think.

But then I remember how I'm in trouble with Ms. Marshall. Not only that, but everyone in the whole class knows it. In fact, since I am brand-new at this stupid school, trouble is the only thing they know about me.

I hope Mommy doesn't find out. She has enough problems already. Everyone says so.

"I'd better clean up this awful mess," I say in my boomy echo voice. I wipe-wipe-wipe at the soap, but the towels only smear it around. I told you they were crummy. And now there is a bigger awful mess to clean up.

"I'd better get busy," I say in my loudest voice. I wipe-wipe-wipe some more.

"I *thought* I heard someone talking," a grownup's voice says, making me jump about a mile in the air. She has skinny little glasses that hang down on a chain like a necklace. They bounce when she talks. "What are you doing in here, honey?"

"I—I'm washing my hands," I say. Hah! And Daisy thinks *she* is the only good liar in the world.

"Well, I think they must be clean by

now," the woman says, spying all the soap bubbles in the sink and the big crumply pile of paper towels.

"Okay," I say.

"I think you'd better get back to class, young lady," the woman says.

First I was honey, but now I'm young lady. That means I'm about to get in trouble again. Even *more* trouble, I mean.

Like I didn't have enough problems lately.

"Okay," I say again. I start to leave.

"Throw away your towels first," the woman says. "And next time don't use so many. Towels come from trees, you know."

"Okay," I say for the third time, and I throw away the towels. But I don't believe her about the trees. That's just dumb. Leaves come from trees, and apples come from trees—I've seen them growing. But towels? Who is she trying to fool?

She watches me walk back to Ms. Marshall's class, so there is no escape.

Ms. Marshall looks at her watch in a cartoony way when I sit down. This is to let me know that I have taken too long in the restroom. I don't care, though, because it is almost time for recess.

It has finally stopped raining, so we are allowed to go to the playground if we put our sweaters on first. Going outside is like getting out of jail, which is where my daddy is now, with all the bad guys.

Which is scary, because my daddy is *not* a bad guy.

Almost everyone in my class starts running around like crazy on the playground. Stevie Braddock comes up behind me and jabs me in the back with his finger. "Ooh, *bus-ted*," he says, like I knew he would. But he is smiling when he says it, and Marcus is smiling too.

Oh, great, I think. Now the worst boys in the first grade want to be friends with me. This was not exactly my plan.

I decide to practice my skipping. Skipping is something a person can do alone. Also, it is the next best thing to running, which is what I *really* want to do. I want to run as far away from Ms. Marshall and Betsy Ross School for Stupid-Heads as I can.

Step-hop! Step-hop! It is hard to get it

right when you skip. When I think about it too hard, my feet go *Step hop-hop!* or *Step-step hop!* by mistake, and my feet get mixed up.

I keep on trying, though. I want to skip down the sidewalk someday when I am with Case and Mommy, and they are just walking. People will turn and stare at me. They will ask each other, "Who is that amazing famous girl?"

Oh, no—someone is trying to catch up with me! I can hear whoever it is getting closer. I'll have to skip faster. *Step-hop!step-hop!step-hop!* I don't want to trip over my own feet.

A hand grabs my shoulder. "Hey, slow down," someone says. "Gee!"

I turn around. It is LaVon, who is the

best skipper in the whole first grade. I was skipping almost as fast as LaVon! "Wha—what do you want?" I ask her. I am trying not to sound like I am out of breath. Because LaVon is never out of breath.

"I wanted to give you this," LaVon says, and she pulls something little out of her pocket. She puts it in my hand. It is Lilanna's other shoe! "We found it in the hall on our way out to the playground," LaVon says.

I look down at my hand. Now I have a tiny red shoe, but I don't have Lilanna any-more! For once I don't know what to say.

But LaVon does. "Me and Daisy are really sorry about what happened to your doll," she says. "We didn't want that to happen. Daisy just wanted me to see it."

"I would have shown her to you," I say, "if you had asked me to."

"Yeah, but Daisy knows you better," LaVon says. "She's the one with all the friends."

Wow—LaVon thinks that Daisy and I are *friends?*

"Look," LaVon says. "She's sorry too." Across the playground Daisy lifts up her hand and waves. LaVon waves back. I wait a little, but then I wave too. "The bell's about to ring," LaVon says.

So we skip back to where Daisy is standing. Everyone is lining up to go back to class. "Hi," Daisy says, and then she turns to LaVon. "Did you give her the shoe?" she asks.

"Yeah," LaVon says. She is smiling.

"I'm the one who found it," Daisy brags. "It was right outside the door. It's so cute!"

I close my fingers around the little shoe in my pocket. It *is* cute, I think. I try to remember the rest of what Lilanna is wearing, but it is hard. Something red.

Then I think about what it would be like to be shut inside someone's locked desk drawer until Friday. Scary—that's what it would be like! I try to count on my fingers how many days it is until Friday, but I keep losing count. Does today count?

Does Friday count?

I try *not* to think about Ms. Marshall, who by now thinks I am nothing but trouble. That gives me an achy feeling inside, because I wanted to have a new start, like Mommy says. Also, now Ms. Marshall will probably never let me go alone to the restroom ever again. I don't want to think about that, either. Instead I will think about LaVon and Daisy, who might be my new friends at Betsy Ross School for Maybe-Nice Kids.

Getting into trouble is a weird way to make friends! I never could have thought of that plan, not in a hundred hundred years.

I miss Lilanna, but I will see her again pretty soon. And real-live people are better than a doll any old day.

But I am still a little bit sad.

Lilanna shouldn't have to suffer just because of me.

CHAPTER SEVEN
Knock, Knock!

"Knock, knock!" I say after dinner, pretending to knock on Case's curtain. He is sitting on his bed drawing, like he always does.

"Who is it?" he asks.

"Come on, Case, you know it's *me,*" I say.

"Me who?" he asks again. Case is really weird sometimes.

"It's me, your sister, Lily," I say. I decide to leave off the part where I usually say *"duh."*

"You may enter," Case says, talking like a king.

It is so great inside Case's hidey-hole, especially at night. He has his own radio on a little table near his bed, and a reading light, too. There isn't room for anything else. It's like a secret cave in there.

I wish *I* had a place like that, just for me. Instead I have to share a room with my mommy. It's not fair!

"Sit down," Case says, so I do. "So what's up?" he asks.

I make my face put on its most serious look. "I got in trouble at school today for the first time," I say. When I hear these sad words come out of my mouth, tears start to dribble out of my eyes. "A *lot* of trouble," I say.

"I told you it would get harder after the first week," Case says. "I'm just surprised it took you so long." He says I can cry at the drop of a hat, whatever that means, so he doesn't care much about my tears.

"Case, quit it!" I say, trying to keep my voice quiet. "This is serious. I'm the only girl in the whole first grade to get busted, and everybody saw me! And I can't tell Mommy, you know that."

Case laughs. "Okay, so what did you do?" he asks. "Hog all the Play-Doh?"

I can feel my face get hot. "No," I say, "that was in kindergarten. This is first grade, and it's *serious*. I broke a stupid rule."

"What rule?" Case asks. "Did you talk without raising your hand first? Did you push to the front of a line?"

"I would never do that," I say. "Not at

Betsy Ross, where I'm making a new start and the teacher thinks I'm sweet. Or she used to, anyway."

"So what did you do?" he asks me again. He hands me a Kleenex.

"I brought a toy to school. A doll. You know, Lilanna. But not to play with," I say in a hurry, "just to show Daisy Greenough."

Casey groans when he hears Daisy's name, but when I glare at him, he holds his hands up like he is saying "Okay, okay."

"So you wanted to show Daisy your doll, but you guys weren't going to play with it at school?" he asks me.

"Right," I say. "But then Daisy swiped it to show to LaVon. And when she gave it back to me, I was the one who got caught with it! And so now Ms. Marshall

is keeping Lilanna for the whole week, until Friday."

"She sounds pretty strict," Case says.

"Yeah, and she shut Lilanna in a drawer, where she can't even breathe. And then she even locked it."

Case doesn't pay any attention to that part of my story. "So you're really mad at Daisy?" he asks.

"No," I say. "Daisy is my friend!"

"Huh," Case says. "Then you're mad at that other girl, LaVon?"

"Nuh-uh," I say, shaking my head. "She's my friend, too." Case just doesn't get it!

"Well, then, who are you mad at? Your teacher?" he asks. He looks like he is about to kick me out of his hidey-hole.

I shake my head *no* again. "Not exactly," I say. "I mean, I *was* kind of breaking her dumb rule. A little. But I'm mad because… because I wanted to be Sweet Lily at my brand-new school. And now I'm not good anymore!"

Case looks surprised. "But you were *never* good," he says. I start to get mad, so he keeps on talking, fast. "I mean you're *good*, only it's deep down inside."

"Ms. Marshall thought I was good right on top, too," I say, sniffling. He gives me another Kleenex.

"Well, that's because she doesn't know you, Lily," he says.

My own brother tells me this! "Well, thanks *a lot,* Casey!" I yell.

"Is anything the matter in there?"

Mommy calls from the bedroom. She is folding laundry.

"No!" Case and I say at the same time.

"Don't tell her," I whisper to Case.

"Okay, but why?" Case asks. "It's not like you never got in trouble at school before, Lily."

All of a sudden I can feel new tears following the old ones down my cheeks. It's like now they know the way. "Yeah," I say, "but I got in trouble at my old school when Daddy got in *his* trouble. I really messed up there at the end."

"I didn't do so great myself," Case says. He has a gloomy look on his face now. Oh, well, at least I am not the only sad person in the apartment anymore.

"Yeah, well, I bet you didn't spill glue all over the floor during creative playtime, accidentally-on-purpose," I say. "And I bet you didn't hide the kick ball at recess so nobody could play."

Case laughs a little bit. "You did that stuff?"

I nod my head. "And a lot more, too. Why, what did *you* do?" I ask him.

Case thinks for a minute. "One thing I remember is that I took this cool book the teacher was reading to us in class," he says, "and I sneaked it into my backpack. I took it home. I told myself I just wanted to see how the book came out, because I wasn't sure I would be around to hear the end of the story. You remember, things were so crazy then."

I nod, but I can feel my eyes get big. "You stole a book?"

"I *borrowed* it," Case says like he's correcting me. "I sneaked it back into class the last day of school. But before that, everyone was looking all over the place for the book. I felt kind of bad, but then I thought, hey, why should they get to have everything? So it felt good, too."

"You were mean," I say, smiling a little. I never knew Case could be so mean!

"I did worse stuff than that," Case says, almost bragging. "Remember Tony?"

"Your friend before we moved?" I ask.

"He *used* to be my friend," Case corrects me. "But when Dad got in trouble, Tony started talking about it behind my back all the time. You know, like he'd ask me questions and pretend that he was all sorry and everything, but then he'd go and tell everybody what I said. So I punched him out after school one day."

"You *hit* him?" I ask. We aren't allowed to hit. Mommy always says to use our words instead, except not *some* words.

"Yeah, sure I hit him," Case says, only looking a little bit sorry. He rubs his hand like it's still sore. "He had it coming. But the point is, I was messing up then, just like you."

"I didn't want to mess up at my brand-new school, though," I say. I can feel my chin start to get all wobbly again, which is my secret sign that I'm about to cry.

"It's not that big a deal, Lily," Case says.

"Yes, it is," I say. "Now I'll have to be bad all year long!"

"*What?*" Case asks. Like I said before, sometimes my big brother just doesn't get it.

I give a big sigh to show him how dumb he is being. "I wanted to be good at Betsy Ross, but now everybody thinks I'm bad," I say real slow. "So I have to be bad."

"No, you *don't*," Case says like he's the one talking to a baby.

"Yuh-huh," I say.

"Nuh-uh," he says. "Lily, you don't have to act all one way or all another way. You can just be—oh, I don't know. *Normal*. Can't you act normal for once?"

"But when I act normal, I always get in

trouble," I say. "Like what happened when Ms. Marshall took my doll."

Casey thinks about this. "Yeah," he finally says, "but once you get the doll back, you can start all over again. Not trying to be all fakey and super sweet," he adds in a hurry, "but just…normal. Or maybe a little better than normal. That would be good."

"It won't work," I tell him. "All the kids saw me get in trouble. I mean, Daisy and LaVon like me now, so that part of my plan worked, but everyone else in my class thinks I'm as bad as Stevie and Marcus. And Ms. Marshall will expect me to be bad from now on. Forever and ever, amen."

Case fiddles with his marker. "Did you tell her you were sorry?" he asks.

I think back and remember almost throwing Lilanna at Ms. Marshall, I was so mad. But did I say I was sorry? "Not exactly," I say.

"*Are* you sorry?" he asks.

"Yeah," I say.

He laughs. "Lily, are you sorry you got in trouble, or are you sorry you broke the rule?" he asks.

"Well, *duh,* both of those things," I say. "But I still think it's a stupid rule."

Case pretends that he doesn't hear what I say about the rule. "I think you should tell your teacher you're sorry, Lily," he says.

"And maybe she'll give Lilanna back to me right away," I say. I am starting to get excited. This sounds like a great idea!

"No, she won't give you your doll back early," Case says like he is some magic guy who can tell the future. "That's the punishment for breaking the rule. But at least she'll know you care about being good. I bet she'll give you another chance."

"Really?" I ask him. "Even if I think her rules are dumb?"

Case laughs. "Well, you don't have to tell her *everything*," he says. "Just tell her you're sorry, that's all."

"Okay," I say. "But I can still think what I want. I'm the boss of my own self, Case."

Case sighs so hard that his drawing paper flutters. "I know, Lily," he says. "Believe me, I know."

CHAPTER EIGHT
Breathing Deep

It is Tuesday, and I can't talk to Ms. Marshall alone until nutrition break.

Finally, it is time. Everyone is outside running around and eating their snacks. Daisy and LaVon want me to play with them. I tell them I will play in a minute, but first I have to do something.

Ms. Marshall is sitting on a bench in the sunshine. She is breathing deep, like the yoga lady on TV. I walk up to her and she jumps a little. "Oh, hi, Lily," she says. Then she sighs a little. "Want to sit down?" she asks, patting an empty place on the bench.

"No, thank you," I say, very polite.

"Did you want to talk to me about your doll, Lily?" she asks.

I nod my head. "Kind of," I say. This saying you're sorry stuff is even harder than I thought it would be. I *hate* saying I'm sorry!

"Well, I'd like to give you back your Barbie doll now, Lily, but remember, you broke the rule. She's in the drawer until Friday."

I don't say *anything* about how dumb I think the rule is. Casey would be proud of me! "I know," I say. "I don't want her back early. But her name isn't Barbie, it's Lilanna." The part about not wanting Lilanna back early is a lie, but so what?

"Lilanna," Ms. Marshall says, her voice all soft. "What a beautiful name."

"Not Barbie," I say again, just to make sure she knows. "Don't call her Barbie when you play with her, okay?"

Ms. Marshall laughs a little bit. "Lily, I'm not going to play with your doll," she says.

Oh, sure, I think. "It's okay if you do," I tell her. I take Lilanna's lost red shoe out of my pocket and give it to Ms. Marshall. "But could you put this back on her? It got lost."

Ms. Marshall puts the little shoe on one of her fingers. "Okay," she says. "I can do that. Anything else you want me to do for Lilanna?"

It just takes me a second to think of

something big. "I wish you could unlock the drawer and keep it open a little bit," I say. "It's hard for her to breathe in there. And she didn't do anything wrong."

"Hmm," Ms. Marshall says. "You won't try to sneak her out of the drawer early if I open it?"

I shake my head and make a big X on my sweater. "Cross my heart," I say. "But it wasn't Lilanna's fault I broke the rule. Why should she be punished?"

Ms. Marshall shakes her head too and looks at me with sparkly eyes. "I guess I never thought of it that way," she says.

"I'm sorry I was so bad," I say. "I want to be good from now on." It's easier to say this very important thing to Ms. Marshall when she might not be listening all the way.

But she *is* listening to me. "Oh, Lily, honey, you're not bad," she says. "You made one mistake, but you're not *bad*."

"Well, I broke the rule, though," I say. For some reason I am thinking of my daddy when I say this. I stare down at my red sneakers.

"Yes, and I'm punishing you for it," Ms. Marshall says. "But I still like you, Lily. I like you a lot! And I just know we're going to have a wonderful year together."

It is cold out, but I can feel my face getting hot. I am thinking four things:

1. My brand-new teacher at my brand-new school likes me, even though I broke a rule.

2. And after I am punished, I can start over again!

3. And Ms. Marshall thinks this will be a wonderful year.

4. And I can see Daisy and LaVon watching me from across the playground.

My new friends wave at me and smile. *Maybe Betsy Ross Primary School isn't so bad after all,* I think.

"Time to go back to class now, Lily," Ms. Marshall says, getting up.

Daisy and LaVon come skipping over to us. "Are you in new trouble?" LaVon asks me, her voice all whispery and serious.

"Nuh-uh, it's okay," I say, shaking my head. I give her a great big smile. "Just the same old trouble as before."

"Phew, that's good," LaVon says.

We get back to class and sit down. And right before we start on our words, Ms. Marshall looks at me, smiles, and holds up her hand. Lilanna's little red shoe is still on one of her fingers!

Ms. Marshall unlocks her desk drawer, pulls it open, and reaches inside. I know she is putting Lilanna's shoe on her foot.

Then Ms. Marshall winks at me. She shuts the drawer—but not all the way. She leaves it a little bit open so Lilanna can breathe.

Pretty soon it will be Friday.

And after that it will be a whole new week.